For my father-in-law Peter Monteferrante

Not Quite Swords for Hire

A Chronicles of Ringworld Novel

Chapter 1

Mercenaries

In Malga, a lone adventurer strolls into the local tavern in search of employment. The tavern was a good place to drink, but also a great place to find freelance work if you had a set of skills that traditional jobs didn't require: the kind of work that either promised fame and fortune, or a premature death. The adventurer, clad in thin leather armor and a dagger hanging from his belt, sat down on a crudely fashioned barrel that doubled as a stool at the bar.

The adventurer looked down the bar and locked eyes with the tavern owner: uninterested in serving an unfamiliar face, the barkeep broke away from the stranger's gaze and pretended he didn't see him there: the locals in Malga weren't exactly hospitable to travelers.

A few minutes passed and the traveler realized that the man behind the bar was intentionally ignoring him: he rose and began attending to his *real* objective. He stood and looked around the tavern, spotting several potential and dangerous looking employers: on the other side of the bar sat a large man with scars running down his face, and only one leg. With no other option, that seemed like good place to start. The stranger made his way down the bar, passing the barkeep who intentionally looked down as he passed. The trail worn-traveler approached the one legged man.

"Hail, friend," said the stranger. It sounded more businesslike than he intended.

The man ignored him and continued nursing a mug of some foamy and foul smelling liquid.

"Perhaps I should come back: it seems like I've caught you at an inopportune time," said the stranger apologetically.

"Leave and keep on walking: and don't bother coming back," said the man, still staring straight ahead and raising his glass to his mouth.

"Pardon?" the stranger was confused and taken aback by the one-legged man's poorly mannered response.

"Let me give you a friendly piece of advice..." The man looked up from his mug and at the stranger: he was more hideous up close than from a distance. "People from Malga don't like strangers: travelers like you looking to find work is what ruined this town in the first place. I'm not a patient man, so I'll only say this once: it might be better for your health if you left in a hurry. Get my meaning?"

The stranger looked at the man for a moment and returned to the barrel he called a seat. He began surveying the rest of the tavern from the bar: he would have to choose his target more carefully next time to avoid a similar situation. The traveler turned back to the bar, futilely waiting for the barkeep. After a moment of waiting, he noticed a scruffy-looking man with a sword draped from his belt arguing with an older gentleman wrapped in a cloak. Several times, he observed the scruffy-looking man put his hand on the hilt of his sword when the argument became heated. Sensing the chance to turn a profit by coming to the older man's aid, the stranger left his seat once again.

Before the scruffy-looking man even noticed, the stranger darted behind him: what was even more surprising is that he managed to lift the sword from its sheath without alerting the enraged mercenary.

"I suppose you'll quiet down now that I've liberated your bargaining chip. No sense in starting a fight you're completely unprepared to win: eh?" the stranger lectured.

"Return that to me this instant, you damned thief! This has nothing to do with you," yelled the irate man.

"I'm afraid it *does* concern me: a bit more than you know," the stranger smirked.

Something long and blunt struck him in the back, knocking him to his knees: it was the one legged man. He struck the traveler with a piece of wood he fashioned into a crutch.

"I thought I told you to get out of here: now I'm gonna let this fella beat the tar out of you. I'll let him soften you up for me," laughed one leg.

During the exchange, the older man in the cloak sighed loudly: so loud, in fact, it could be heard over the arguing.

The irritated man picked his weapon up off of the ground and returned it to its sheath: he then grabbed the stranger by the collar and lifted him off the ground. He hoisted the strange traveler and let out a powerful punch. The man dropped the strange traveler and quickly fell to his knees, holding his fist and yelling out in pain.

"Imbecile," grunted one leg as he raised his crutch to strike the traveler down.

The stranger's one legged assailant began to bring the crutch down, when some unseen force knocked the attacker against the wall hard. The other assailant followed him into the same wall.

The man in the cloak lowered his arms, fixed his cloak, and crouched to help the "injured traveler.

"I could have handled that myself, but thank you all the same. I appreciate the thought behind protecting a harmless old man. My name's Edgar, by the way," said the cloaked man.

"Paul," grunted the sore traveler.

"Well then, Paul... please join me for a drink. Allow me to help you over to my private table," said Edgar, supporting Paul under his arm and leading him to a table off in the corner. "Now, tell me... what brings you around these parts? An adventurer like yourself doesn't just wander in here without a purpose."

"You're right," Paul was beginning to regain his composure. "I was looking for work in this town, but found a fight instead."

"You're pretty fast to have gotten that sword away from that mercenary without him even noticing," Edgar remarked.

"Fast, but not incredibly durable I'm afraid. You could probably tell from that little display back there," Paul explained.

Edgar snapped his fingers, and the barkeep that had been ignoring Paul all night promptly brought him a mug filled with a dark colored beverage.

"I suffer from a distinctive lack of durability and speed, I'm afraid. Ask a wizard to do something from a distance, and he can take care of it without a problem: but give him any other task and... well... you get the idea. Let me get right down to business..." Edgar started: he had Paul's undivided attention.

"I need something recovered for me: I'd do it myself, but this requires speed, stealth and strength: three fields in which I am obviously lacking. Take care of this task for me, and I will reward you for your time," offered Edgar.

Paul sat and stared and considered taking on this unknown task."One question: what exactly does this entail?" he asked.

"I need you to sneak into Malga Cave and retrieve the staff hidden there," Edgar explained.

"If it's a cave, why do I have to sneak in?" asked Paul.

"The staff allows the person holding it to render himself invisible at fixed intervals. Something that valuable is bound to be guarded by monsters," mused Edgar.

"Okay: I'm in. I'll do it for a thousand gold: half of it up front," Paul's eyes lit up at the prospect of the lucrative venture.

"Two thousand, but only after I have the staff in my possession. I have to make sure you don't run off with the gold before you do your job," snapped Edgar.

Paul suspected that the wizard had been duped in the past. "Alright, we'll do it your way, but I want three thousand upon my return, and I want to keep anything I come across during this venture."

"Deal," Edgar was very agreeable. "I'm surprised you didn't hold out for more, to be honest."

There's a certain professionalism that comes with this trade: don't refuse what other adventurers can do cheaper. " But there's still one minor thing... You mentioned speed, stealth *and* strength. Well, I have two of those covered already," Paul said.

"I planned on that. Paul, meet the other adventurer I hired in town," Edgar waved his hand, and a warrior wearing a full suit of armor stepped forward. “Paul: meet Devon. He’ll be providing the muscle on this trip.”

Devon extended a hand towards Paul. “Pleased to meet you.”

“Forgive me if I’m not overly eager to make friends, but I have a rule in this line of work: never get too close to the people you adventure with. That makes it easier to deal with any on the job "accidents”. All the same, nice to work with you,” Paul extended his hand and shook Devon’s.

Edgar smiled to himself. “Excellent: it seems like the two of you will get along fine on this job. The cave is just outside of town: if you leave early in the morning, all you have to do is follow the rising sun and you’ll find it without a problem.”

Chapter 2

Slow Walker, Fast Talker

The next morning the two adventurers, under the employment of the wizard, departed for the cave. As the wizard Edgar had suggested, they left at first light: Devon, still tired from a night of drinking at the tavern, reluctantly followed Paul out of town and towards their target.

"Gods, you move slow! I'm the one who drank entirely too much last night, yet you're the one who's moving at a crawl: weren't you hired for your speed?" despite his headache, Devon still mustered the energy to taunt Paul.

"We're not being paid by the hour here: we're getting paid for results. Why waste valuable energy that we'll no doubt need when we get to the cave? Besides: do you really think it matters to the wizard if he gets his staff this afternoon or tonight?" Paul abruptly halted and turned towards Devon. "And by the way: if I remember correctly you were hired for your strength. How do you expect to defeat *anything* when you only got a few hours of sleep last night? Before you try to make an observation about someone else, you should take a look at yourself." Paul returned to walking: his speed was slightly faster than before.

Devon shrugged off Paul's comments. "At any rate: I can see the cave off in the distance. I'll keep my end of the bargain and cut through anything that gets in our way: just try not to get into too much trouble."

"I should say the same to you..." Paul muttered under his breath.

The two continued to walk for quite some time in silence before they reached Malga Cave. The cave was no different than any other run of the mill cave: the entrance was a large archway in the side of a rock wall with no one to guard the entrance. Devon was the first to begin making his way inside.

"Stop, you idiot!" Paul grabbed Devon's arm and tugged him back rather violently. "Are you new to this, or are you just stupid? You *NEVER* walk into an entrance of someplace that supposedly houses rare treasure without first checking for traps."

Paul picked up a long stick and gestured at a thin, almost invisible tripwire running across the bottom of the entrance. "There's a reason that this place seems deserted: they have a trap to handle any unwanted guests." Paul used the end of the long stick to push the tripwire down.

A click sounded, followed by silence.

"See? There was nothing to worry ab..." Devon was cut off by a barrage of arrows that crashed down from the ceiling of the cave.

"*Now* it's safe to go in. That's one you owe me," Paul chided.

"How did you know that would be there?" Devon asked.

"On the job training: you learn to detect these thing quickly or your 'career' can end in an instant," he answered.

"Help me here: I've never had to deal with traps before," Devon was almost pleading.

Paul's eyes lit up, and you could see the gears in his head moving. "I can, for a nominal fee."

"I'm listening," Devon began reaching for his gold pouch.

"It's simple: from this moment forward, I get to decide whether I want to keep any of the treasures we will undoubtedly find inside. Furthermore, I reserve the right to keep all of the gold we receive in exchange for any of the items we come across. Just sign here..." Paul pulled a piece of parchment and a feather pen out of his vest. Deception was one of his finer talents.

Devon signed the contract without ever having read it.

Paul smirked, rolled up the parchment, and returned it to his vest. The two mercenaries then made their way further into the cave. As Paul predicted, the first few halls of the cave were laden with traps: one particular trap sent a sharp log hurtling their way which they both barely sidestepped. Of course, the cavern also had its fair share of valuable treasures: Paul claimed them all as Devon had suspected.

After finding a few treasures, Paul was bogged down with the weight of his ill-gotten gains. Dragging a large amount behind him caused him to trip a few arrow traps by accident: needless to say, he easily avoided them all.

"I think it would be safer if I held on to the treasure for now," Devon offered in fear of tripping more traps.

"That sword and armor make you heavier than me. If you want to try, be my guest..." Paul began handing Devon some of the more cumbersome items, like the mace they found.

Devon opened his pants and slid the mace down. Before Paul could stop him, the weapon had disappeared entirely. The mace, of course, was much longer than Devon's leg.

"How did you?" Paul was astonished.

"It's called a 'pocket dimension'. Basically, they may look like a pair of pants on the outside, but inside there is an amazing amount of space. That's how I carry all of my gear: do you think this is my only sword?" Devon explained.

"...I have no doubt that you didn't come up with that yourself," Paul said flatly.

"Nope: won it in a barroom bet. Best bet I ever made," Devon said with a look of satisfaction on his face. "But forget that right now: I hear something."

The sound of scratching could be heard in the chamber they were in, but the darkness coupled with the echoes of the cave prevented either of them from pinpointing the source. Devon's hand quickly moved to the hilt of his sword.

From behind them, a small Wolf-like creature pounced and landed on Paul's back. Devon reacted quickly, drawing his sword and swinging in an upward arc. Devon cleft the creature in two, but nearly hit Paul in the process.

"You *idiot*! You nearly got me instead!" grunted the irritated thief.

I aimed before I swung... besides: no harm done, right? On the bright side, that thing didn't have the chance to do any damage to you," Devon rationalized: he knew his aim was off in the darkness.

"Let's just keep going: the sooner we get the staff to the old wizard, the sooner we can put all this behind us," Paul spat.

As luck would have it, the chamber they were in opened to a larger room lined with several torches and well lit. In the corner of the room was the staff that their employer had undoubtedly described to them. As they entered the center of the room, a low growl became audible.

"I don't think we're alone. Devon, you act as the distraction while I grab the goods and make a run for it," Paul whispered out of the corner of his mouth.

Devon nodded in affirmation: he drew his sword and prepared to do battle with whatever was lurking in the room. Paul made a dash towards the staff, but was tackled to the ground by a large, and very hungry looking Warg. The beast was several times the size of the one that pounced on Paul's back earlier, and at least twice the size of either of them.

Paul landed hard on the floor of the chamber and managed to scramble his way out from underneath the huge wolf before the beast could swipe at him with its enormous claws. He got to his feet with much difficulty and kept heading in the direction of the staff. From behind, he could hear the sound of Devon pouncing on the beast and launching an attack. He did not envy Devon in the least.

Paul turned to run to the opening leading out of the chamber, but was blocked by Devon and the Warg. He carefully sidestepped around the two combatants and promptly broke for the exit. At the foot of the archway Paul stopped and looked down, listening to the struggle behind him. At extreme risk to his own safety, he turned and drew his dagger.

Just as Paul turned to assist Devon, the Warg fell to the ground with Devon's sword plunged deep into its neck. With a sigh of relief, Paul simply offered a "good job" to the exhausted warrior.

"That's my job: to keep things like this off of you long enough to finish the job," Devon gasped, trying to catch his breath.

"You didn't have to risk your life: you could have just run when you had the chance," Paul shook his head and grabbed the staff. Appearances aside, he was actually grateful to the mercenary he happened to be paired with.

"One more thing: when we get back to the tavern in Malga, I'm buying." Devon said, not realizing that the contract he agreed to earlier entitled Paul to all the gold they got in exchange for the treasures of the cave: the staff included. Devon wouldn't have the money to buy a round of drinks even if he wanted to.

Paul simply nodded in agreement: tired from the trials of the cave, he wanted nothing more than to get back and rest. The two exhausted warriors made their way out of the cave and prepared for the trip back to Malga.

Chapter 3

Thin Air

Paul and Devon made it back into Malga by nightfall: the sun had just set, and the tavern was at its peak of business. Though Paul could be sneaky, devious and underhanded, he was a man of his word: tonight, he and Devon would celebrate their victory, and the following day, he would depart for the next town before Devon woke. Even he had to admit, for someone he considered an idiot, travelling with the mercenary had its merits: Devon possessed the best traits of a brick wall and a pack mule while being able to offer the occasional, albeit infuriating, conversation.

According to their employer, he could be found at the same table at the tavern when the two returned with the staff in hand. Surely enough, the older gentleman sat at the very same table in the corner of the bar: along with the wizard, two pouches filled until the seams came close to splitting sat on the table. Paul began calculating how big a travelling pack he would need in order to carry all of his gains on the trip.

"Ho there, brave adventurers. I trust you have returned victoriously?" greeted the wizard.

"Well, it was no easy task, but here is the staff we promised. At great risk of life and limb, might I add," Paul said, hoping that their employer would include a bonus.

"Excellent work: I've got your reward right here, but first, let us drink," the wizard snapped his fingers and gestured toward the barkeep, summoning him over with five large mugs of some sweet smelling liquid. "Drink up lads, we'll conduct our business soon enough."

They spent the next few hours celebrating at the wizard's behest: drink flowed and stories were shared, mostly about the battle with the Warg. By the time the evening was done, there were several empty mugs on the table: surprisingly, Edgar had consumed none of them. He nursed the same mug for the entire evening, but certainly ate his share of bread.

"Now gentlemen: allow us to complete our transaction. I believe you have something for me?" Edgar was smiling widely.

Paul motioned to Devon, and the warrior retrieved the staff from his "storeroom". Partially baffled and mortified, Edgar confirmed the staff's identification just from looking at it.

"Gentlemen, if I may confirm that it isn't a replica, we can complete our transaction and you can be on your way this evening," Edgar politely insisted.

Devon nodded and handed the staff over to his employer.

"This is indeed the proper staff. I know you went through a great deal in order to retrieve this for me, so allow me to give you an added bonus," Edgar smirked.

Paul's eyes unconsciously widened.

"I appreciate your hard work. Here's your tip: be careful who you trust in future dealings," Edgar took hold of the staff, nodded, and vanished.

There was no trace of where the wizard had gone: at least, none that Paul or Devon could find. Paul quickly grabbed at the pouches on the table, and rocks fell out of both. The two had fallen for the wizard's trick, and fallen hard.

Paul rose from his seat quickly, and Devon sluggishly followed. Together, they burst through the door to the tavern and into the night air. Outside, not a sign of the wizard could be found: the only person either of them encountered outside was the barkeep, who had come outside after them. Though he hadn't said two words to Paul during his trips to the tavern, he had no problem expressing his anger at the two of them trying to skip out on the exorbitant tab. As a parting gift, Edgar had left the rather large bill unpaid.

"There has been a miscommunication, and I can both understand and appreciate your frustration. You see: my travelling cohort and I were under the employ of a patron of yours. Perhaps you remember him? A tall and gangly older fellow by the name of Edgar," explained Paul.

"I make it my business not to get to know the patrons: if he was paying, then I was serving him. Making friends with your customers ends in situations similar to this one. Now: this bill isn't going to take care of itself," demanded the barkeep.

Paul begrudgingly nodded at Devon, signaling him to give the man what they had found in the cave.

"This should just *barely* cover the tab. I'll let you go, since I'm in a good mood but let me be clear on this one thing: I never want to see either of you in my tavern again," the man from the bar said over his shoulder as he walked back inside.

Paul sat on the edge of the wooden steps leading up to a general store next to the tavern and looked up.

"No worries Paul: we can just replace that using the money we get from Edgar when he returns," Devon offered.

"You moron: he never had any intention of paying us. It was a scam, and we fell for it. Well, at least I can say I'm not surprised that *you* fell for it," Paul sighed.

"I'm not entirely stupid: I didn't give the barkeep *everything* we found. According to our agreement, it belongs to you," Devon pulled out a small gold anklet.

"Devon... keep it. We both wasted our time: you might as well walk away with something to show for it," Paul pushed the trinket back towards Devon.

"The joke's on you: I signed a contract, remember?" Devon once again held the trinket out to Paul.

Paul let out a long sigh. "You dope... tell you what: at least hold on to it for me."

That night Paul slept out under the stars while he let Devon rent a room at the inn using the anklet they found. He truly felt bad for Devon: he was a tough fellow, but easy to take advantage of. Paul got to thinking that he was exactly the kind of person he needed to travel with to barrel through obstacles.

The next morning, Paul waited outside the inn and Devon was late to rise, as usual. Devon was a bit surprised to see the thief that morning: based on his explanation the previous day, he thought that Paul would have moved on to the next town by then.

"Come on: we're wasting time just waiting here, and half of the day is gone already because you slept so long. Shape up and get moving, or this is going to prove to be a long trip," Paul joked.

"I thought you made it a rule to work alone?" Devon asked, still surprised.

"Don't make me regret breaking that rule. Actually, I'm already starting to… let's just get going," Paul sighed.

"Where are we headed next?" Devon asked.

"Well, the Thieves Guild here isn't exactly welcoming me with open arms anymore… professional disagreement of interpretation: apparently they take the saying 'honor amongst thieves' seriously… anyway… we're not exactly well liked here, so our next mark is Alaris, to the north. Alaris is a trade city, so the odds of us finding good work there are pretty high," Paul said sheepishly.

Alaris lay beyond a vast forest about a day's travel north of Malga. Many powerful wizards and various collectors called the trade city home: if you were looking for something mundane, the odds were that you could find it in the marketplace. If you needed something rare and hard to find, the black market was the best bet: there was no doubt lucrative employment to be found there as well.

"Do you think we'll ever run into Edgar again?" Devon asked as they walked into the horizon towards Alaris.

"For his sake, I hope we don't. Why?" Paul responded.

"If we do, he still owes us three thousand gold each," Devon said.

"Devon."

"Yes Paul?"

"Please don't say anything for a while".

Chapter 4

Black Market of Alaris

Alaris was a very large city with a population as diverse as it was dense: unlike most villages its size, Alaris was *not* a castle town, meaning there was no castle to contribute to its size. The town was formed by thieves and murderers over the course of a century: the abundance of ancient ruins nearby provided a plethora of artifacts for adventurers willing to brave the unknown to retrieve them. Magical items fetch a high market price, and, as anyone in Alaris can tell you: money talks. In time, the small camp that was Alaris turned into a market, and that evolved into a small settlement: it further evolved from there as more and more "collectors" arrived and invested money in town.

There was no "good part of town" to speak of: if you had the desire to make someone disappear and the money to do it with, willing mercenaries and assassins could be found anywhere in town. Alaris had a city council, but it was mostly for show. All in all, a great place to lose all your money, and an even better place for an adventurer to find odd jobs.

"So, this is Alaris?" Devon marveled at the sheer size of the town. From the entrance, the spires of some of the more fantastic buildings could be seen rising into the sky.

"It is indeed, and the next place I planned on looking to make a name for myself. I've never actually been here before, but..." Paul paused as a cloaked fellow walked past a patron of a fruit stand and took his coin pouch without rousing his targets attention. "... It makes me wonder why they have a Thieves Guild in Malga and not here."

"Where exactly do we start looking? From the sheer size of this town, I'd say the tavern would be a great place to start," offered Devon.

"Under normal circumstances, I'd say you're right: but, the *real* money is in the Black Market. All sorts of rare items that have been... questionably obtained... from all over Ringworld eventually end up here. On top of that, this area is abundant in ancient ruins that are teeming with valuables that no one is using right now: private collectors are always hiring teams to go in and raid those ruins. They *are* dangerous, after all," Paul explained, pushing his way through a crowd of people.

"How dangerous are we talking?" Devon's attention was grabbed by a stranger passing by. "Hey, was that an Elf?"

"Well, to answer your first question: the more valuable the treasures are, the more dangerous the ruins. There's really no way to tell until we get there though. To answer your second question: it probably was. People of all races and backgrounds congregate here: some because they have something they're looking for, and some because they've been shunned by their people." Paul looked up at the horizon. "It's almost dark: that means we don't have long to wait. We can go to the tavern as per your request, but do me a favor: tuck you gold pouch away and don't let anyone see it. It looks like some of the locals have wandering hands worse than I do."

"Actually..." Devon lifted his pouch and held the empty piece of fabric upside-down.

"Hmmm... we seem to have a bit of a financial issue: I.E., we're broke. Well, if we play our cards right that won't be an issue much longer," Paul sighed.

The two wandered deeper into town and through the slums: they eventually came out in front of a large building with two spires rising into the air that resembled a church. Upon closer inspection, it was a private residence, and a rather extravagant one at that.

The sun had disappeared behind the horizon, and all manner of men gathered outside of the central market: from well dressed gentlemen to slovenly shopkeepers. Many of the men carried pieces of paper. After observing for a few moments, many other travelers like themselves showed up and usually ended up conversing with the various "vendors" there.

"Watch... just observe for now," Paul instructed. He put a hand out to gently to block Devon.

"What exactly are we watching for?" Devon asked: he had never seen this done before.

Paul sighed. "It's simple: we watch to see how many people accept the jobs available. The one with the least amount of takers is the one to go with. If you want to make a name for yourself, you have to be willing to take the jobs that no one else will: coincidentally, those are usually the highest paying."

"What about that one?" Devon pointed at a small group of people gathered by a rather obese man holding a piece of paper.

"Well, that *does* have the fewest... ok: don't say I never take your advice seriously," Paul said, but in actuality he planned on going over to that group anyway.

The two hesitantly walked over to the group of adventurers, looking all around them and taking in the interactions between the mercenaries.

Paul approached the fat man with the paper and put on his most charismatic façade. "Good evening, sir. My name is Paul, and my associate here is Devon: we're professionals in the "import and export" business looking to find employment as we pass through these parts."

"I can always use an extra pair of hands. Tell you what: I'm putting together a team of adventurers to delve deep into a tomb that has, until recently, been undisturbed. Rumor has it that it is the tomb of a powerful wizard: but what do rumormongers know? If you work well on a team, you're welcome here," muttered the obese man.

"But Paul, I though you said you work best alo..." Devon found Paul's elbow in his ribs before he could finish the thought.

"With a group of highly specialized adventurers!" Paul yelled over Devon's remark.

The fat man paid no attention to this and handed a rolled piece of paper to Paul.

"This is a map of the top floor of the tomb: it's the only floor that has been explored so far. That's my last copy, so I can only offer you one. I'll pay you based on what you return with, but be warned: you may be part of a team, but this is every man for himself. You only get paid for what *you* bring back," the man blurted.

Paul shook his hand and walked off to a corner near the group with Devon.

"You didn't have to hit me so hard..." Devon held his ribs where Paul struck him.

"Yes... I did." Paul laughed to himself.

Not understanding Paul's humor, Devon shrugged his odd comment off. "One quick question though... we're in the import and export business?"

"Well, yes. We import things that people aren't using, and export them for a profit: import and export." Paul replied.

"And if he had asked you about your experiences as a thief?" pushed Devon.

"I thought of that too: I had a fake list prepared." Paul said with a great deal of satisfaction.

Devon rolled his eyes at the thief. "And if he didn't believe you?"

Paul smiled. "I always keep an escape clause at the bottom of the list when I'm in too far: the escape clause involves a dark alleyway and the tip of my dagger."

"And you say that *I* don't think things through..." Devon said under his breath.

The two waited there for about an hour when the group began to move. The pack leader, a smaller man in a grey cloak, led them out of town and through a field. There was no moon, so it was particularly dark that night: as a result the footing was treacherous, making for a long journey. After a great deal of walking, the cloaked man brought them around to a large hole in the ground, large enough to fit several adventurers through at the same time. He lit a torch revealing a staircase that he promptly descended. The others quickly followed leaving Devon and Paul outside.

"This doesn't feel right, but here it goes. Money is money, after all, and you *do* have to eat sometime..." Devon's voice was shaky from nerves. He followed the group shortly thereafter.

Without a word Paul followed Devon down the stairs. Inside, the narrow staircase opened up to a cavernous hallway made of stone blocks. Devon drew a torch from his pants and lit it, trying to decipher the map that his employer had given them all the while.

"This thing is useless: it's almost a straight shot to the first flight of stairs, and there are no traps on the first floor: according to the map, at least." Devon rolled up the map and added it to the rest of his belongings.

"Come on: we want to catch up with the group before we get too far behind," Paul commanded. "Try to wedge yourself into the center of the group."

"Why the middle? Wouldn't we want the front to we can grab anything we come across before the others do?" Devon had a valid point.

"Think ahead: yes, the people in the front will pick up the most treasure, but they'll also be the first to set off any traps or deal with any monsters. Who do you think will be the next to pick up what they drop?" Paul didn't give Devon much time to answer. "On occasion, a trap will catch you by surprise from behind: that also ensures that we'll have protection at our backs."

"I'll trust you on this: I've never travelled in a group before, so I don't know how this works," Devon replied.

The two continued walking down the poorly lit hall.

"Neither do I: that just seems logical," Paul said

They caught up with the group right before reaching a stone staircase leading into the depths of the unknown.

Chapter 5

Deep Within the Tomb

They worked their way towards the center of the group: there were about eight adventurers present aside from Paul and Devon. As they descended the staircase, the overpowering stench of must coupled with decay hit their nostrils: a smell that Paul was all too familiar with in his line of work. Familiar or not though, it's the kind of smell that you never get accustomed to.

As Paul had predicted, the traps of the tomb began to whittle away at the group almost immediately: a pressure plate on the stairs opened a pitfall a few steps ahead of it, claiming one of the larger warriors. That was commonplace on excursions like this one. The more experienced adventurers treated their fallen comrade like an insect bite-insignificant. The two who panicked were obviously inexperienced and, very likely, the next to go. Not surprisingly, they were the two young-looking chaps in the back: they couldn't have been much older than eighteen or nineteen.

The hall bent to the right and one of the treasure rooms of the tomb was uncovered. Upon entering the room, dusty jewels, golden goblets, and other items, no doubt magical in nature, were immediately visible. One of the younger men from the back pushed his way past Devon and began pleading with one of the larger, more experienced looking mercenaries: Paul and Devon couldn't hear much of the conversation from where they were, but Paul was able to guess based on the bits and pieces that he picked up, and the speed with which the two youths in the back ran away.

Before the two ran off, the adventurer he was talking to handed him a rather mundane looking chalice: Paul guessed that they exchanged their share of treasure on the trip to avoid returning empty-handed, or to ensure they returned *at all*.

Devon managed to get his hands on two of the rings that were scattered about on the floor, but as he clasped them in his hand, they made a loud popping sound, and promptly shattered.

"Magical items tend to explode when you put them together: my guess is that you didn't know that. Why do you think you never see wizards wearing more than three rings on each hand?" Paul's last question was more rhetorical.

Devon tossed the pieces of metal aside and continued on through the room. The adventurers at the front had already taken anything of value: the room was empty.

Paul nudged Devon with his elbow. "Now we wait. Hopefully there are no more pitfalls."

"What if they all make it out?" Devon whispered.

"They won't: trust me. From the looks of things, there isn't a skilled thief among them: they won't be able to spot the traps before it's too late," Paul replied.

"Morbid way of turning a profit..." said Devon under his breath.

Paul caught Devon's statement: "That's the way thieves are: we're like scavengers that take poach the prize after the hard work has been done."

A scream rang out from the floor above them. As the group exited the first room, they froze, waiting for something else to follow.

Nothing, save the sound of wood crackling from the torches, could be heard.

"What do you suppose that was?" Devon asked, still frozen in place.

"One of those idiot kids probably ran into trouble upstairs: odds are we'll find his body on the way out," said a voice from the front of the group.

They continued to creep down the hallway: though one of the fellows narrowly dodged a bladed pendulum that came down from the ceiling but he didn't see the spear coming when it rose from the floor. They were down to four of the original eight: Paul's biggest regret was that the poor impaled fellow didn't have anything of value on him when he died.

Devon saw something shining in the wall from the corner of his eye: as he crept closer, he saw a gem the size of his fist covered in dust in a recessed shelf in the wall. So as not to draw attention to himself, he continued to creep towards the jewel at a steady pace. Devon was only a few steps from the jewel when Paul turned to look for him.

Paul shook his head vigorously in an attempt to stop Devon from moving any closer, but alas, he shook his head in vain. Devon was now within reach of the gemstone: his foot came down slowly.

Click

A low grinding noise could be heard coming from somewhere in the tomb: the shelf that was holding the large jewel also opened and let the stone drop.

"What were you thinking?! Do you want to get us killed?!" Paul whispered harshly.

"I figured that it was something worth grabbing: we don't want to leave with nothing to show for it," Devon whispered back.

"Listen: rule number one is to *always* be sure to scout the area first. Making sure it's safe before you act is invaluable. Rule number two is to forget rule number one if someone else is there to act like fodder. Let them get it, because the odds are that you'll be taking it off of their corpse soon enough," Paul was whispering so fast that most of his words ran together. "Just be grateful that nobody else heard that grinding sound."

Devon looked to his right and saw the orb of torchlight surrounding the other adventurers disappearing around a corner.

Paul sighed. "It would be in our best interests to keep up with the rest of the group: safety in numbers and all that..."

As the two lollygaggers sprinted to catch up with their travelling companions: the orb of torchlight came to a grinding halt. The hallway before them turned, but this time, there were two separate directions to choose from. Both hallways extended too far to be able to see with mere torchlight, so the adventurers began wandering down the path to the right.

The hall was very plain: the stone walls that lined the rest of the tomb extended further down the hallway. The odd thing about this path was that there were no doors, turns, or branches: the corridor just continued to extend in one direction. At the end, something could be seen shining in the darkness. As they got closer, a gold bracelet adorned with jewels materialized on a pedestal. The bracelet was, no doubt, very valuable: the two men heading the group thought so as well. They began running and contending with each other to see who could reach the treasure first: the man on the right tripped over something and was sent flat on his face into the darkness.

As the bearded mercenary fell, Paul could hear a sliding noise: the man by the treasure disappeared into the darkness as he reached the pedestal. A few moments later, a scream could be heard below them.

Paul came forward and slowly approached the pedestal: as he moved forward, he came to an abrupt halt as the ground disappeared below the tips of his toes. The other fellow competing for the treasure undoubtedly fell on a pressure plate, opening the floor.

"There's no way forward," Paul called back to the remaining two and Devon. "We have no choice but to turn around and go down the other path."

They backtracked their way to the split in the passage and took the other route, which led to another long and dark path.

"So much for staying towards the center of the group: we pretty much *are* the group now," Devon said to Paul: they were now in the back of the small band.

"A lot of pitfalls here: stay focused and watch your step," Paul whispered.

"We can't be far from the main tomb, right? There's bound to be enough for all four of us to leave with our arms full," Devon complained.

The four came to a dead end, with a large stone plate on the floor. The two mercenaries in the front lifted the stone plate and leaned it against the wall.

"Don't look now, but I think we still have more to go..." Paul said to Devon.

Another staircase leading down into darkness stretched out before them. In an attempt to see how far they went down, one of the remaining men tossed a torch into the darkness: the torch disappeared, and a cold, foul smelling breeze came through the opening.

"That's concerning..." Paul muttered to Devon under his breath. "Why don't you go first? My constitution is lacking..."

"And you call me an idiot..." Devon retorted.

"I prefer the term cautious," Paul chuckled.

With their two companions in the front, the four descended the staircase into the cold and windy corridor below. As they descended the stairs, a scratching sound could be heard deep within the tomb, though its exact location couldn't be determined.

Chapter 6

The Sound of Defeat

"Paul..." Devon whispered.

The thief paid no attention to Devon and continued his way down the dark and drafty stairwell.

"Paul..." Devon said slightly louder.

"Hm?" was the only acknowledgement Paul would give him.

"Something here isn't right: I know it. I may not have been at adventuring for as long as you, but even *I* can tell when we're in over our heads. Paul... are you even listening?" Devon was carefully watching his step so as not to activate any hidden traps. "Paul?"

Nothing but silence came from Paul for a moment. "... I'm trying to concentrate Devon. Stop acting like a coward: you remember that got those kids from earlier," he snapped.

Paul carefully stepped over a tripwire with a pressure plate beneath it: a double trap meant to trick those who saw the wire coming.

"Watch your step: try to land a couple of steps past the tripwire so you don't set off the one beneath it," Paul instructed.

Devon and Paul carefully made their way down the stairs and into the hallway below. The third basement floor was unnaturally cold: the wind coming from deep in the tomb put out two of the torches. Only Paul's and one of the adventurer's remained to cast a dim light on their path.

They crept down the hall, which slowly changed from brick to carved out stone, searching every room along the way. There were far and few chambers along the walls: that floor was, for the most part, a straight hallway. Paul halted his progress into the dark and turned toward Devon: Devon, however, was only a shadow in the distance. He had stopped some time earlier to examine something.

"Devon: don't dally or you'll get left behind! The last thing you want to do down here is get lost in the dark: you'll never find your way out," Paul said, trying to keep his voice down.

"I was just... never mind. On my way," Devon called out in the darkness.

As Devon hurried down the hallway to catch up with the others, he heard the same scratching noise that he heard earlier. He looked around to see if the others had heard it, but they paid no mind. Old tombs were full of creaky sounds, after all.

"Did anyone else hear that scratching?" Devon asked: the question was directed at whoever was listening.

"I didn't hear anything, and besides: if you heard something it was likely some animal burrowing through the ground on the other side of these walls," Paul attempted to reassure him, but reassurance was not Paul's strong suit.

"This far underground? We started out pretty deep to begin with, but we went down two more flights of stairs since we started." Devon began to worry.

"Listen: Frost Wurms tend to burrow deep within the ground: that's probably all it was. Quit complaining and concentrate on keeping your eyes peeled," whispered Paul.

Paul was so focused on telling Devon to watch his step that he forgot to watch his own: as he ended his sentence he stepped right on the center of a pressure plate. Paul quickly hopped back a few steps, froze and looked around to watch for incoming arrows or a spear rising from the floor. After a few moments of silence, a grinding noise could be heard in the wall, followed by another cold gust of wind.

"What happened?" asked Devon, puzzled at Paul's sudden movements.

"I *may* have slightly miscalculated my stride and the interval of which the constructor of this tomb placed his deterrents..." Paul trailed off.

"You stepped on something you weren't supposed to: didn't you?" Devon gathered from Paul's speech.

"You can't prove that," Paul quickly retorted.

The scratching sound echoed in the tomb again: this time, it was loud enough for Paul to hear. The other two adventurers must have heard it too, because they both turned toward Paul and Devon with quizzical looks on their faces.

Paul elbowed Devon to get his attention. "Call it 'adventurer's intuition', but I think we should be going... *NOW.*"

The group of adventurers turned to the exit and began the speedy egress from the tomb. Paul and Devon led the group on the way back up: they were in such a hurry that neither of them was concerned with placing fodder in front of them. They made it as far as the staircase when another gust of cold and foul smelling air blew in from behind them.

Everyone quickly turned: before them stood the inhabitant of the tomb, and no doubt the source of the scratching noise. Their employer had been right about one thing: it *was* the tomb of a powerful wizard. Before them floated a decayed wizard: he had been sealed up for so long that he was mostly skeletal.

The words coming out of the Lich's mouth echoed in the dark hall. "You have done well in making it this far. I should thank you for freeing me from my prison: a deed I shall repay with death. Thieves: feel my wrath."

With a mere wave of its hand, the bearded mercenary at the rear of the party fell down dead.

Paul nearly pulled Devon's arm out of the socket as he yanked the warrior up the stairs behind him.

"Even though that chap has obligingly died leaving us all of his treasure, I'm afraid we'll have to decline: sticking around here will result in certain death!" yelled Paul.

As they ran up the stairs, Devon's shin pulled the trip wire that they had stepped over earlier: several compartments opened in the wall, letting out a barrage of arrows. The arrows all missed them, but the Lich continued to follow the three with a great deal of arrows sticking out of its side.

From their side, Paul and Devon both noticed orange rays whizzing past them: the Lich was hurling spells in an attempt to stop their escape. After several poorly aimed bursts, the Lich succeeded in hitting the last adventurer, or as Paul so aptly put it: their last line of defense. The ray hit the adventurer in the shoulder, sending him tumbling to the ground. The Lich stopped his pursuit to make its way to the downed adventurer. Paul and Devon did not slow their hasty escape for even a second: rather, they took that opportunity to get as far away as they could.

"This could be going better!" Devon yelled to Paul.

They reached the staircase leading from the second basement to the first. They could hear the sounds of screaming coming from behind them.

"Run faster! I think our distraction has expired: if you don't want to end up the same way, then *move*!" Paul jumped to the ground from the stairs so as not to lose any momentum.

Another orange ray narrowly missed hitting Devon's head: the Lich was back on the chase. The undead wizard was quickly closing in on the two: Paul and Devon could see the light of dawn shining in from the end of the hall. The Lich began reaching out its rotted hand...

The pursuit suddenly stopped and Paul, along with Devon, began running up the stairs into the fresh air of the great outdoors. The two burst outside and collapsed to the ground: both of them struggled to catch their breath.

"By the gods! We barely... made it out... with our lives..." Devon panted.

"I know... that was most... unfortunate..." Paul managed to get out.

They sat by the entrance to the tomb catching their breath and basking in the warm glow of the sunrise.

"So... that's it then: a night of adventuring followed by extreme terror only to come out of this empty handed. What a waste of talent and time," reflected Paul.

"What do you mean?" Devon asked.

"We have nothing. Another of my brilliant plans: completely fruitless." Paul seemed genuinely upset at their venture.

"We didn't get out of there *completely* empty handed." Devon began to smirk.

Paul looked up at Devon to see what he was going on about, and he was holding up a book with several gems in the cover.

"How did you...?" Paul's mouth was hanging open in amazement.

"Back in the tomb when you left me behind in the third basement: I saw this outlined in the dark, so I took it and pocketed it before anyone could notice," Devon explained.

"Do you have any *idea* of what that is?" It didn't matter how Devon answered: Paul was going to explain it one way or the other. "That Lich was wizard in life: as a wizard, he likely had a spell book containing the incantations that he mastered. That's what you're holding."

"And here I thought that the gems might be worth something. I guess we're lucky I grabbed this thing" Devon laughed.

"When the man who hired us sees this, we'll get more of a reward than either of us could have imagined. The gold will keep us well fed for a very long time." Paul started wringing his hands together.

The two returned to Alaris the very same day and spent the afternoon searching for their employer: it turns out he was a private antique collector. The fat man cared more about the book than what Paul and Devon had to go through to get it: he cared even less about the loss of life in the labyrinth. He paid the two quite handsomely for the book, with an added bonus for keeping the incident under wraps should anyone come looking for them.

Chapter 7

Crimson Eye

Based on their success in the Lich's tomb, Paul and Devon continued to work together. The gold was abundant: they were far from rich, but they always had enough to keep themselves fed, clothed, and indoors. Several years passed, and a partnership eventually formed.

The two had worked with each other on a plethora of freelance assignments: together, they retrieved artifacts of notorious repute, defeated monsters, and were banished from their fair share of towns. Paul and Devon's personalities seemed to mesh: mostly because Devon was a brick wall and Paul didn't hesitate to take advantage of that fact.

A high success rate eventually gave the two a sense of what jobs were worth taking and which weren't: this saved a lot of time and wasted effort in the long run, but it also bred a certain kind of arrogance. That arrogance led them to pass up some opportunities that would have brought them unimaginable wealth and fame: that very same arrogance blinded them towards employers who would end up taking advantage of them in the end. All for the sake of their vow never to find themselves in the employ of a wizard again.

For years the two had heard stories and rumors about a gem of unparalleled beauty. The Crimson Eye, a ruby red gem the size of a clenched fist, was the focus of many fables, failed expeditions, and slain adventurers. Long before Paul and Devon met, rumors whispered in dark corners of taverns spoke of the gem's location: like many legends and stories of Ringworld, the location of the gem and details of the story would change each time. Paul heard these tales since he first started out as an adventurer, though he never took them seriously: that is, until the stories started synching up.

A previously unexplored labyrinth had been discovered deep in the woods near the Clarian Region: an ethereal looking fortress appeared out of nowhere one day in an area that was already well explored. Many adventurers and prospectors speculate that the labyrinth belonged to some sort of wizard, and that it appeared once the spells concealing it disappeared, meaning that the owner was probably dead. Though many have tried to enter the fortress, the strange sounds and inhuman howling coming from within have turned away more than its fair share of brave adventurers. It was rumored that the legendary gem rested within those walls.

Paul and Devon worked odd jobs in the Clarian Region for some time: there was always money to be made, and as long as there were unexplored ruins around, somebody was going to want something "liberated". It was a very lucrative time for adventurers willing to put their lives on the line. With the construction of new settlements in the Region, new ruins and tombs were being uncovered at a consistent rate.

New stories and employment opportunities swept through the Clarian Region like a wave: Devon and Paul frequented one of the many nameless taverns in the area in hopes of riding that wave to greatness.

Devon peered over his half empty mug at Paul from across a table in the center of a tavern. "It's been close to a week and we haven't gone out for any jobs: not that I'm complaining. We have more than enough money to hold us over for a while, but, I'm getting restless just sitting here."

"Patience. I already told you it's senseless to go out for jobs that don't yield anything. Besides, if we waste all of our time running around on fool's errands we'll miss all of the big jobs," Paul replied, putting down his empty mug.

Devon brought his mug to his lips, and then brought it down to the table again, emptying the rest of the liquid in the thick glass in a single gulp. "That's not how Vargas sees it, I'm sure. He's our biggest competition, and he got where he is by taking all the jobs we wouldn't."

Paul turned towards the entrance and responded with his back turned. "Beginners luck: if he had any *real* skill he'd stop picking up our droppings. He's just a scavenger…"

Devon set aside his empty mug. "But I thought you said *we* were scavengers?"

Paul pretended not to hear Devon and started listening to the conversation at the table next to them.

A short and rather filthy man whispered to the other two adventurers at the table adjacent to Paul and Devon. "I'm telling you: this is it! Why do you think there are so many noises coming from inside that new keep? Because there's something there to protect: that's why. That's the reason nobody has found it yet."

The cloaked man sitting across from the dirty adventurer responded, but most of it was inaudible. The only thing Paul could hear was something about a red stone.

"Crimson stone..." the filthy adventurer said. The other two immediately told him to lower his voice.

"I've heard that it has some sort of power, and that anybody who possesses it is granted wonderful and unnatural abilities," said the adventurer sitting next to the cloaked man.

"Bah: fairytales, I say. This isn't worth our time! We pay you for information: not stories. Don't waste your time, or ours. Bad enough you're wasting our money," the cloaked man was obviously irritated.

"It's not a waste of time! I heard that Vargas himself has taken an offer from one of the locals and has gone there searching for the gem. If we could... if *you* could beat him to it, just imagine how much that will help your reputation," blurted out the dirty man.

Paul turned back towards Devon. "Well: it turns out that waiting around paid off. As it just so happens, the Crimson Eye itself is rumored to rest in that labyrinth they just uncovered. ," Paul whispered.

Devon stared blankly at Paul. "The what now?"

"The Crimson Eye. That's the fourth or fifth story I've heard about it being in that fortress, so there must be a shred of truth to it. It's something that people have been talking about since I was a boy: probably before that even..." Paul tried to recollect all the stories he hear regarding the gem. "From what I understand, it's some sort of ruby-like gem the size of your fist and is supposed to be magical or something."

"So it's just a ruby?" Devon still looked puzzled.

"It's not so simple: the stories say that the Crimson Eye is some sort of gem that has yet to be identified. It has an intense clarity to it: so much so that it makes regular gems seem mundane. Even *if* the stone doesn't have 'magical powers', I'm sure it would be worth a lot to a collector. If we found that, well, we could retire from the adventuring business, or at least choose the adventures we want," whispered Paul. He tried to keep his voice down in case there was another person like him that was trying to eavesdrop on the conversation.

"I'm still not convinced... it sounds like a story to get idiot adventurers to go off and die," Devon observed.

"Should be right up your alley: the idiot part, I mean. Oh, and one more thing..." Paul smiled to himself. "I heard Vargas has already taken the job from someone. I *suppose* we can let him find the stone and keep the fame and fortune to himself."

Devon didn't like Vargas very much: he though Vargas was arrogant and insufferable.

Paul found Devon's bane. "I can tell from your expression that you want to get out there and do some searching. Well, first thing is first: we have to find a willing 'donor' to fund our trip into the unknown and to pay us for our troubles."

"So I suppose it's pretty much decided then? You know what that means..." Devon trailed off.

"No: what?" Paul asked.

Devon raised his hand and motioned towards the bartender. "Another round!" he called out.

The bartender promptly responded to Devon's request and brought two large mugs filled to the brim over to the table. The fact that Devon and Paul were some of his best patrons probably had something to do with it.

Devon raised his glass toward Paul. "How hard can this really be?"

Chapter 8

Like a Fox

As soon as Devon brought his mug down from the toast he consumed the contents in a single gulp: after finishing, he brought the glass down hard on the table.

"The question remains: where are we going to find someone to fund this treasure hunt? I'm sure that collectors and the like aren't exactly lined up for something that may not even exist," Devon observed.

"That's the beautiful part: we slip in, grab whatever we can, then we get out of there. Even if we don't get our hands on the Crimson Eye, once people find out we ventured into the labyrinth, *they'll* come to *us*," Paul explained, and rather loudly.

A slight increase in his volume was all it took: a disheveled looking older gentleman at the table across from them turned his head toward Paul and cleared his throat. Paul locked eyes with the stranger, and in the next few moments, the stranger rose to greet Paul face to face. The man seemed clumsy as he walked over, narrowly missing the bartender who passed by him with an arm full of empty mugs.

"Speaking of the devil..." Paul muttered to Devon.

"What is it, Paul?" Devon glanced over at the disheveled stranger heading their way.

"I don't know for sure but... we're about to find out," Paul finished, and the strange man approached him.

"I'm...ah... I didn't mean to overhear or anything... but... ah... well, I'm looking to get a few things from that new labyrinth you see... and well...

uh... I heard you talking about it and..." The man said hurriedly.

"And... you want our help: is that it?" Paul said impatiently.

"To get to the point? Yes. I'm a... peddler of sorts... I buy things that adventurers get from old ruins and I... sell them at a *slightly* elevated price. More importantly... I can probably get a high price for most of the things in that fortress... there was, after all, some kind of enchantment on it. The odds are there are some pretty valuable treasures in there... on top of that... I have heard rumors that the Crimson Eye is inside," muttered the stranger.

Paul was getting aggravated at the older gentleman's slow, stuttering speech. "Let's talk business then: how much are you willing to part with for each item we retrieve? After all, these are our lives we're risking."

"I'll determine what each item is worth *after* you bring them to me. I'll pay you well, I can tell you that," responded the strange man.

"Can you guarantee that?" asked Devon.

"I can do one better... I can put it in writing." The strange man pulled out a yellowed scroll. "This guarantees, in writing, that I'll compensate you market value for everything you retrieve."

Paul grabbed the scroll from the strange man and started reading to himself. "Contractual obligations.... Market value... termination conditions... failure to return... seems legitimate."

Paul and Devon both signed their names to the scroll.

"Alright... now let's get down to business..." The man's demeanor changed from clumsy and timid to confident and manipulative. "You're working for me now: and you'll continue to work for me until I say so."

"Wait, wait, wait. That contract we just signed *clearly* states..." Paul trailed off as the strange man waved his hand over the scroll revealing more writing.

"If you had bothered to look at the back, you would have seen the sigil I put in the corner to hide the ink. As you say, the front states the terms you agreed to *very clearly*: but the back nullifies the first part of the contract and changes the terms. In short: you only work for me now. I want that Crimson Eye," the man grinned, revealing a mouth full of crooked, discolored teeth.

"What makes you think we'll honor this contract?" demanded Devon.

"Let's see... how should I put this... this is no ordinary piece of paper. This scroll is enchanted with a soul link: that means that as long as it bears your signatures, I'll be able to find you wherever you go. Think of it like a compass," the man grinned again. "Take a look at your arm."

A sigil appeared in red on Paul and Devon's right forearm.

"And what makes you think you pose a threat to either of us?" Devon was starting to lose his patience with the man.

"I have been known to practice the arcane: I can make life *very* uncomfortable for the two of you." The strange man raised his hand and snapped his fingers: the surface of the table across from them burst into flames. "I think I've made my point, gentlemen."

"So, what do you want from us exactly?" Paul demanded.

"I need adventurers to go out and get some things of... importance..." the stranger trailed off.

"And you needed to con adventurers into doing your bidding?" Paul spat.

"Exactly: the things I need are in places no sane adventurer would set foot into. A skilled treasure hunter would never accept such a job, and someone crazy enough to go is obviously lacking in the skill department. I've had my eye on you two for some time: it's obvious you have the skill. The only other adventurer that came even close to rivaling your reputation is probably rotting somewhere in the labyrinth right now," explained the man.

"So you're the one who employed Vargas... the joke is on you then: he's all talk and no skill," laughed Devon.

"That's exactly why I waited for you two. Spread a few stories about the treasures inside the fortress in the woods and watch them take the bait. The only thing I had to do was frequent this... establishment..." their new "employer" chuckled.

"Exactly what's so dangerous about this dungeon? There's something of incredible value inside too, no doubt: besides the Crimson Eye, that is." Paul was actually starting to show intrigue.

"There are plenty of things inside, but what I want is what you already mentioned: the Crimson

Eye." The disheveled looking man turned toward the entrance. "As you may have already guessed, the fortress belonged to a wizard: an old rival of mine. I could never pinpoint where he made his home because of the spells he used to conceal it, but something recently appeared out of nowhere. I used the fodder... Vargas, I believe... to go in and confirm that it was the right place."

"That's all we have to do then? Get in and out with the Crimson Eye and you'll let us out of the contract?" Paul inquired.

"Dear me, no." The stranger with the bad teeth started laughing to himself again. "Under this agreement, you're basically slaves. I have further use for you: if you return alive, that is."

Paul glared across the table at the con man: his eyes were full of a deep enmity. When the strange man finally left, Paul and Devon sat in silence for some time: perhaps it was in disbelief that a fast one had been pulled on Paul of all people, or perhaps it was the fear of wandering into a dungeon that even the most powerful wizard wouldn't set a foot into.

Devon reflected on Vargas' fate: though the two of them were more skilled than Vargas could ever hope to be, the fact that he fell victim to the labyrinth so easily did not sit well with him. Exactly what was inside, who was this wizard and why did he go to such great lengths to keep intruders out? Even more disturbing were the thoughts of exactly *what* lengths he went to.

Sleep didn't come easily to either of them that night. They each spent hours pacing back and forth in their respective rooms. Paul eventually slipped into his armor (for safety reasons) and went for a walk through the settlement to clear his head. He was met by the sounds of crickets chirping noisily in the night: their sound was like laughter to him, mocking his foolishness earlier. For him, it wasn't the fear of venturing into the unknown (although that *did* have something to do with it): it was the fact that someone had conned him so easily, being a fast talker himself.

Paul came to a four-way road in the middle of the settlement and decided to turn right, taking him past the tavern. He slowly walked past, staring intently at a stranger turned toward the tavern entrance. After a few moments, the stranger outside the tavern finally turned towards him. It may have been his imagination or some kind of arcane trickery, but for a moment he saw the stranger that scammed them earlier, staring at him and tapping his finger against the very scroll he and Devon signed just a few hours ago.

Paul shook his head, looked away, and looked back again. The person he mistook for the con man was a tall, thin bearded gentleman who paid no mind to the strolling rogue. Considering his exhausted state and the fact that navigating the fortress would probably take a great deal of energy, Paul returned to the inn and prepared for the next day's ordeal.

Chapter 9

Enigma

Paul and Devon awoke and met downstairs early the next morning: they both seemed tired, but each seemed *more* eager to get their quest over with. What was supposed to end in fame and fortune was turning into a nightmare: the treasure of legend, the Crimson Eye, was their instrument of enslavement, not salvation. Paul swore the entire morning that he was done looking for jobs from other people, and that he and Devon would do entirely freelance work from there on out. If someone needed something, Paul and Devon would find it on *their own*: no more contracts, bounties, or getting into situations that were beyond their abilities.

Devon was normally a talkative fellow, but that morning he was silent. Lack of sleep coupled with the sensitive subject of their enslavement gave him nothing to chat about.

The night was just beginning to turn to dawn when the two left the inn. Leaving early was a rule that Paul insisted on: over time it rubbed off on Devon. Entering a cave or labyrinth at that time of day ensured that any nocturnal creatures waiting for a hapless victim were ready to slumber, and that any day dwelling creatures were still groggy from previous night's sleep. At the very least, leaving early ensured that they would be travelling while it was still cool out, allowing them to conserve energy rather than travelling in the heat of the day.

The mysterious fortress was not far from the settlement Paul and Devon came from. tit was a relatively short walk to the north and a small distance into the forest. As they stood at the entrance, a flight of stairs leading into an abyss, and a group of black birds flew from the trees above them.

"That doesn't bode well," Paul said, looking down the stairs.

"Let's just get this over with," sighed Devon.

The labyrinth itself rose from the ground up to about Paul's knee: the silent fortress obviously stretched far underground. Paul glanced over at Devon and began to approach the stone stairs, slowly descending them.

"If you have a light or a torch, now would be the time to use it," Paul called up to Devon.

"As luck would have it..." Devon began rummaging around in his pants leg. "I have one magically enchanted torch left. The flame from this torch burns as bright as daylight: the only drawback is that it burns four or five times faster than a normal torch."

Paul stopped and turned back toward Devon. "Well: I guess we'll just have to move fast then."

Devon hurried down the stairs to where Paul was waiting and ignited the torch. As the merchant promised Devon, the torch burned as bright as the sun: an added bonus was that it gave off a white, ash-like substance that could be used to backtrack their way outside. A normal torch costs somewhere in the range of a few gold pieces depending on the availability of the oil used to soak the tip: this particular torch cost him several thousands of gold. Hopefully, his investment was worth it.

The staircase led far underground: neither of them could be sure, but it felt like they walked the entire length of a small stable on the way down. At the bottom Paul looked around for signs of where they should go first: the scratch marks in the ground leading to the left-most passage indicated that most adventurers went in that direction.

"Any thoughts on which way is right? Remember, there *is* no map to follow this time: it's all instinctual. This is where those dungeon navigation skills will come in handy," said Devon.

"I think we should go left," answered Paul.

Devon looked down the hall to the left. "Wow: that was quick. What makes you say that?"

"Observation: look down." Paul pointed at the worn away path on the stone floor.

"Fair enough. Come on: we have to be as quick as possible," Devon said, pointing out the small pile of white ash gathering around his feet.

Paul nodded and started to walk down the passage to the left. The hall was lined with pieces of old armor and dusty bones: Paul had a feeling that, while some of these bones weren't as old as the others, they had been here for quite some time. His guess was that small groups of adventurers would wander in here by accident where they met their fate. A large majority of the weapons and armor that lied scattered in the hallway was rusted and completely worthless and entirely unusable.

"Do you suppose..." Devon was cut off.

"Don't even waste your time: they're rusted. Even if there was something worth salvaging, you said it yourself earlier: this torch won't last," Paul spat.

"That's not what I was going to ask. What I was *going* to say was: do you suppose whatever did this is still down here?" Devon said angrily.

That was something Paul hadn't considered: though time would eventually lay waste to even the meanest creature, there was no telling what lurked in the dark depths of the fortress. Though he was usually pragmatic, Paul's imagination began to run with images of abominations: the like of which he had never encountered.

"Stay focused: there's another branch in the path up ahead." Devon motioned down the hall to a split in the distance that was barely visible. "Is that..."

The two continued their way down the hall to the split. Paul and Devon stood and stared at the wall for a few moments, then Paul spoke up.

"This is fresh: we should watch our steps," Paul observed as he looked at a large patch of blood on the wall: several activated traps littered the path to the left.

"Something tells me that's too big for us to get across," Devon pointed to a large pitfall that spanned the hallway from wall to wall, barring their advancement down the left path. "My guess is that whoever it was dodged the other traps, activated the pitfall and then accidentally set all of these off when he tried to dodge."

"This was probably Vargas: he's the only one who supposedly made it this far recently. Here's the more disturbing question though..." Paul pointed at the blood stain and then pointed at the floor. "Where did his body go? There's no trail leading away from this patch of blood: so he obviously didn't walk away from this. That leaves one other alternative..."

"Which is?" Devon asked, worried about the answer that Paul might give.

Paul was silent for a moment and listened for any sounds of distant footfalls. "It means we're not alone in here."

"Well, as much as the idea bothers me, we can deal with it when it comes up. For now though, let's keep moving. The path to the left is obviously out, so we have no choice but to go right," Devon said sternly.

Paul stopped and stared at Devon for a moment, then nodded at him in affirmation. Now, cognitive of the traps that waited for unsuspected intruders, Paul led the way. He moved slower than he did previously: judging from their previous encounter, the traps down here were clustered, creating a deadly obstacle course. Clearing a trap didn't necessarily mean that you were safe.

Paul and Devon made it about halfway down the passage. "Wait!" Paul put his hand out in from of Devon and halted his progress.

Paul pointed out a tripwire in an unusual place: the wire was level with his chest. One more step and he would have activated the trap.

"Hold on a moment..." Paul said absentmindedly.

Paul slowly crouched and looked underneath the wire: as he suspected, there was a pressure plate a step past the trip wire, waiting to claim anyone with the foresight to avoid the first trap. Paul slowly crawled through the tripwire and the pressure plate, revealing three other traps: a large raised plate on the wall to the right, an arrow trap past that, and a stone column protruding from the ceiling that waited to crush intruders. From the end of the hallway, Paul instructed Devon on how to navigate around the traps safely: with a few minutes of careful maneuvering Devon made it through.

"Want to see something interesting?" Paul asked in that tone of voice that said he was going to do something regardless of the answer.

"I know that tone of voice, and it tells me I should be afraid to ask," Devon replied.

"Think about it: we have to go back through here, right? Let's make the trip out easier..." Paul crouched down and picked up a piece of rubble from the corner.

Before Devon could say anything else, Paul tossed the stone into the closest pressure plate.

A stone column crashed down from the ceiling with enough force to smash anyone unfortunate enough to stand underneath it to oblivion. As the room stopped shaking from the impact, a volley of about twenty arrows passed from one wall into the other: as the last arrow disappeared into the wall, a series of spikes came out of the ceiling, pushing down on the pressure plate. A large blade came down from the ceiling and swung in an arc passing through the trip wire: finally, a burst of flame came forth from the floor, fading as quickly as it appeared.

"I know that could have easily killed us: but, you have to appreciate the architecture that went into making this place. A series of traps that activate each other is ingenious: you're not really safe until you get past them all," Paul marveled.

Devon looked up at his torch: the flame had already burned down half way. "We need to get moving: we have one other normal torch after this, but this one is fading fast. Let's get a move on!"

Chapter 10

Burning in the Dark

After slipping past another bevy of traps, Devon watched Paul set off another chain reaction of certain doom. The hallway split again slightly past the second trap fiasco: this time the passages ran to the far left and straight.

"Your guess is as good as mine," Devon said.

"My guess is *better* than yours, actually. Here's a little trick I picked up in Fohn right before we met up in Malga." Paul pointed ahead and started gesturing to the paths. "This is one hundred percent sure to point us in the right direction: the higher-ups at the guild told me so. It's a little something that the former head of the guild developed."

"Former?" Devon asked: a wave of fear washed over him.

"He met an... unfortunate end: he had a 'run in' with an arrow, so to speak. Tends to happen when you fall on a tripwire." Paul's alternating hand started to slow down.

Devon was much more nervous when he heard this. "And you're using something he came up with?! Why do I have the worst feeling about this..."

Paul stopped on the left path. He turned back and looked at Devon as if to say "now that wasn't so hard, was it?"

Satisfied that he was able to apply what he learned in Fohn, Paul started walking down the hallway in a proud, almost forced march. That forced march brought his foot down on a pressure plate.

Well, almost.

The pressure plate slid half way into place when Paul realized what he did. The distinctive "click" telling him the trap was activated hadn't occurred yet: Paul froze in place, afraid to move. Devon called his name from down the hall, but the fear of moving kept him from responding.

Paul started to look around for other traps in his frozen state: if he managed to get off of the trap without setting it off, landing on another switch would be counter-intuitive. Out of the right corner of his eye, he could see a trip wire: the left looked clear as far as he could tell.

Paul slowly lifted his foot off of the plate and threw himself to the left as far as he could: fortunately, the area was as clear as he thought. Devon rushed over to Paul's aid as soon as he landed on the ground.

"Are you alright?!" yelled Devon. "Forget that: what were you thinking?! You could have gotten us killed!"

"Yeah... but I didn't. And on the bright side, my trick worked! We now know which path is the correct one. Told you it works every time!" Paul was chuckling from the shock of almost having died.

"What makes you so..." Devon was cut off by a clicking sound and a pitfall opening in the floor a few feet from where they were. "...sure... Well, you win this round, let's get moving."

Devon helped Paul off the ground and they headed down the other path. The passage was relatively trap-free, and, more importantly, it brought them to a flight of stairs leading deeper into the fortress. After a quick examination, Paul gave the word to advance down the stairs. At this point, only a quarter of the original torch remained.

As they reached the bottom of the stairs, the passage branched to the left, ending in a door, and another passage led forward. Assuming that a dead end would bring them right back to the staircase again, Paul elected that the two go left: of course, the term "elected" is a polite way of saying "recklessly walked off". Devon stopped Paul as he noticed something shimmering at his eye level.

It was a tripwire suspended in the air: the light from the torch hit the tripwire in such a way that it shone a silvery light. Devon noticed something was amiss about this particular trap.

Paul crouched down and looked at the stone door at the end of the hall: he was again amazed at the architecture. The trap was designed so that the door would swing out and hit the wire activating it even if you managed to avoid it. Paul meticulously examined the door to make sure there were no other pressure plates or other traps waiting for them.

"Well, I have good news and bad news," Paul sighed.

"Go on..." muttered Devon.

"This room is rigged so that something bad happens if you open the door, so there's bound to be something good inside. The bad news is that I have no idea how to open it..." Paul stopped and listened: he seemed startled.

"What is..." Devon whispered, but he heard the faint sound of footsteps on the stairs down the hall.

"Whatever it is, it's walking on all fours. From the clicking sounds we hear with each step, I'd say it has some pretty long claws... turn out the light," Paul whispered.

"This is our only light for right now: I don't think..." Devon was cut off.

"I don't care what you think: that light is standing out and telling that thing where we are. Turn it out!" Paul commanded, still trying to keep his voice down.

Devon extinguished the torch by dashing it against the wall: the flame died with a flash of white light. The magical ashes that fell from the torch burned Devon's hand, and he flung the torch into the darkness in reaction to the pain.

The footsteps became faster until they were sure that the creature in the darkness was galloping towards them: suddenly, the sound of the footfalls died, leaving Paul and Devon in the silent darkness.

"Devon..." Paul whispered sharply.

"I'm here," Devon whispered back. The two stood frozen in the dark.

Paul didn't respond right away. "... Do you hear anything?"

"No, I think whatever it is has gone..." Devon replied.

"Do you have the torch?" Paul asked.

I threw it: don't worry though, I have..." Devon reached into his seemingly bottomless pants leg and searched for something flammable. "... a candle... not what I wanted, but it will do."

Sparks flew out from Devon striking pieces of flint and steel against each other: after about five strikes, the wick from the candle ignited. Devon turned to Paul to see how he was faring: Paul's gaze was fixed forward. Devon continued to watch Paul for a moment, then slowly turned his gaze down the hall.

A beast with the body of a wolf and the head of some sort of dragon stood right next to them: the creature somehow managed to sneak up on them in the darkness. Startled by this unnatural hybrid, Devon dropped the candle, and his only source of light. The flame went out as soon as it hit the ground.

Devon and Paul continued to sit in the darkness in hopes that the creature would pass them by. Several moments passed, and the creature finally let out a hiss: the odd beast also let a shower of sparks out of its mouth.

After the sparks subsided, the creature howled and pounced on Devon: fortunately for Devon, its claws glanced off of his armor. It continued to claw at Devon's chest furiously for a moment, then it disengaged to go after Paul. The beast must have had some sort of low light vision: it found Paul and charged at him without hesitating. The creature rammed him and threw him into the wall.

Paul drew his dagger in vain: without a source of light, he was unable to see where his assailant was hiding. A claw passed through his forearm, and something warm and wet started to drip down his wrist.

Devon tried to draw his sword and attack the beast, but a miss resulted in his sword hitting the wall and sending sparks up. The sparks lit the area enough to see that the creature had Paul pinned against the wall. Devon promptly sheathed his sword and dove toward the beast.

Seeing Devon's attack coming, the creature moved out of the way. It again leapt forward and attacked its already injured prey. Though the creature did not penetrate the leather armor that Paul wore, the blow sent him into the stone door.

The beast was on him in a moment, pinning his body against the wall. It let out a growl, and Paul heard some sort of cracking: the next thing he felt was the creature's immensely hot breath. Paul felt around for something to jam in the creature's mouth to keep it from closing its jaws around him: with his uninjured hand he felt around the door. Paul's hand found something small and thin, which he wrapped his hand around and tugged.

Click.

Something rammed the side of the creature, sending it into the wall: that was followed by the familiar "whooshing" sound that can only be produced by an arrow: silence followed.

Several minutes passed and Devon retrieved his last torch: he nervously struck the flint and steel together. The tip of the torch burst into flames, and the orb of soft light surrounded him. He slowly turned to look at what the creature had done to Paul, when he saw the beast in the corner. A large iron spear had come out of the wall and rammed it in its side: a volley of arrows finished the job. The arrows were sunk deep into the monster's body.

Paul sat with his back to the door holding his left arm: blood trickled down his dagger.

"It's a lot worse than it looks. One bandage and I'll be fine," Paul said.

"What was that thing?!" Devon yelled.

"I couldn't say: I've never seen anything like it before. The odds are, that's the reason that adventurers are afraid to go deeper into the dungeon," Paul grunted: his arm must have hurt a little worse than he let on. "We can't relax though: we should get this door open and get out of here before more of those things come."

Chapter 11

Blood Red

The stone doors scraped against the floor as Paul and Devon pulled them open: Devon scrambled to pick up the torch to see what waited for them in the room ahead. Unlike the previous chambers, this one had a very obvious enchantment cast upon it: the floor was coated with a layer of impermeable darkness. In the middle of the room was a pedestal with a red crystal on it.

They had found the Crimson Eye: the problem now was getting to it. Judging from the traps throughout the dungeon, walking through a room where the floor was obscured was not the best course of action.

"There's the target, but: how do we get to it?" Devon stated the obvious, as he was adept at doing.

"I don't know: I don't suppose you happen to have a ladder on you?" Paul asked facetiously.

"That's not a bad idea..." Devon muttered. "... but why a ladder?"

"Well, *something* that prevents us from walking across this floor. You remember what happened back there with that series of traps? The entire floor could be one giant pressure plate: the problem is, I have no way of finding the traps without being able to see," Paul remarked.

Devon held the torch to the ground in an attempt to cut through the darkness: he felt around on the ground at the edge of the field. The ground was most certainly there, his hands confirmed that, but the concept of a blanket of darkness escaped him.

"There's definitely something there: can't we just feel our way across?" Devon asked. He thought this was the most useful idea he ever had.

"If you want to put your hand or foot down in the wrong place and get a face full of iron spikes, be my guest." Paul continued to rub his chin in thought.

"So why don't you skip a few stones into the room to activate all the traps?" Devon asked.

"Because..." Paul thought about Devon's suggestion for a moment. "That's so simple I would have never thought of it. *This* is why I think you're useful: your suggestions are genius in their simplicity."

"I thought it was because I can take a hit and cut down anything in my path?" Devon was asking in earnest.

"That's certainly a close second: now, don't make me regret praising you. Grab me a handful of the largest rocks you can find," Paul commanded.

Devon nodded and disappeared into the room behind them: several minutes later the orb of torchlight began shining into the room at Paul's feet. As he directed, Devon found some *very* large stones: the problem with large stone is that they are often times very heavy.

"Grab these: I think it's in our best interest to be outside this room if something happens," Paul said, grabbing a handful of the smaller stones.

The two quickly retreated from the room and closed the stone doors enough so that Paul could fit his arm through the crack in the center. Paul launched the first stone at the dark floor: he ducked behind a door for cover, but nothing happened. This continued for about four of five stones: then, Paul got lucky with his aim. As the next rock he threw touched the ground, a grinding noise could be heard coming from the ceiling above them: seconds later, a series of sharp iron spikes came out of the ceiling at obscene speeds and extended to the floor in the darkened room.

"*That*, my friend, is exactly why we didn't want to feel around for traps," Paul grinned.

The spikes retracted into the ceiling just as fast as they came out. Devon saw what Paul was doing: he was tossing the stones in a straight line leading to the pedestal in order to clear a path. He had a plan after all: and here Devon thought it was blind luck.

Paul tossed three more stones into the room: the last one landed with a click. Flames rose around the pedestal in the center of the room: they died away after a few minutes and the room was silent.

"Now: this is where you come in," Paul gestured to Devon. He withdrew a rope from his vest. "I'll tie this around my waist. I'm going in: but if you hear *anything* that sounds like it might be a trap ready to go off, I want you to pull me back as fast as you can."

"What if I don't pull you back in time?" Devon was flustered.

"I'll probably be dead, in which case I won't have time to worry about you not pulling the rope fast enough." Paul looked back at Devon. "... Don't let that happen."

Paul did what he did best: he slithered in the shadows, following the line and reaching the pedestal. Devon looked on intently, and Paul slowly reached out to grab the Crimson Eye from its resting place. Paul slowly wrapped his fingers around the gem, and gently lifted it off of its platform.

"I got it," Paul sighed with relief.

Unfortunately, Devon didn't hear him and took his sigh to mean that he was in danger: as Paul wiped his brow in relief he was violently tugged towards the door by his waist. Paul landed a few feet from the door and put his hands out in front of him to keep from falling: his right hand slid across a stone with a click.

"Pull me out you moron!" Paul yelled, stringing most of his words together.

Devon yanked Paul out of the room with all of his strength: before Devon could regain his footing, Paul dove to the side and shut the stone doors as quickly as he could. Seconds later, several objects crashed into the other side of the door.

Paul looked at the door in disbelief. "What were you thinking?! You idiot! I made it through just fine!" Paul's face was red in the soft light that the torch emitted.

"I thought you... never mind that: we're halfway done. We have the stone: now, let's get out of here," Devon said curtly.

As angry as Paul was, he couldn't ignore a good idea, and after everything they encountered in the dungeon, escape seemed like the best idea he ever heard.

Thanks to their previous efforts of setting off the traps and leaving a trail of ash to follow out: their escape was easy. No new traps lay in wait, and no strange creatures barred their path: they did, however, follow the ashes the wrong way, almost falling down a large pit when they came up the stairs. It felt great to be back out in daylight, but their eyes had to do some adjusting after being in the dark for so long.

Paul put his hand in his pocket and grabbed a hold of the gem: he withdrew it and held it towards the light. The Crimson Eye was even more dazzling than the stories described: it was a faceted gem as red as blood and as clear as a mountain spring.

"I won't lie: this is probably the most beautiful jewel I have ever laid eyes on, but I wonder..." Paul paused in thought. "...What's so important about it? Beauty aside: it seems like an ordinary jewel to me."

"Give it here," Devon said, and Paul tossed the Crimson Eye to him. Devon turned it about in the light, "I think we've been had: but who cares as long as we can put this behind us? At any rate, I think we should get back so we can be done with this job."

Paul and Devon spent the next few hours travelling back to the settlement south of the labyrinth. The sheer exhaustion that they felt from navigating the subterranean maze made the return trip feel longer. Though they were usually concerned with attacks from wild beasts, compared to the creature they faced in the dark, a monster or two was nothing.

They made it to the outskirts of the settlement as the sun was beginning to set: as usual, the two made their way to the tavern. The town was unusually busy, and the tavern was full of unfamiliar faces. From what Paul could gather, adventurers from far and wide were gathered there after rumors of the Crimson Eye's location had spread to the surrounding regions. A lot of the travelers gathered there seemed like they would take the Crimson Eye by force, had they known that it sat in Paul's pocket.

Suddenly, a hand touched Paul's shoulder: it was Albert, their captor. Paul was much less thrilled to see him that he would have thought.

"I take it that you have what I require since you returned alive?" asked Albert. Apparently, he didn't believe in formalities.

Paul withdrew the gem from his pocket and handed it to Albert. "Here: now, release us from your crooked contract."

"Release? You've only finished half of the job I had in mind."

Chapter 12

Greed is the Dark Side of Ambition

"What do you mean?" demanded Paul, slamming his fist down on the table beside them...

"It's like I said during our first meeting: should you return alive, I have further use for you. You've returned, and you're very much alive: don't worry though, I'll let you out after this," mocked Albert.

"What's so funny?" Devon demanded after Albert began laughing to himself.

"Nothing at all," replied Albert through small chuckles.

"Alright: let's get right to business. What do you want us to do? " asked Paul.

"Your work ethic should be commended," Albert shook his head. "Let me get to the point then: I'm sure you've heard of the Clarian Volcano... it's been dormant for some time now. Since it last erupted, a Red Dragon has made itself comfortable there, and, as I'm sure you already know, Red Dragons are vicious creatures."

"What's your point?" Paul mulled it over for a moment. "Don't tell me..."

"The other half of the item this gem is a part of is a staff: as a failsafe, the wizard who crafted it hid it away in the dragon's lair in order to deter the wrong sort of person from gaining its power," Albert began.

"So, why not use some other stick? What's so important about this staff?" Devon demanded angrily.

"Let me finish!" Albert snapped at Devon. "Well now... as I was saying: the staff is crafted from a unique material. A Wisdom Tree grows when a wizard transfers all of his life force into a seed: once that seed takes root, it takes several centuries to grow to maturity."

"So, this staff is carved from the wood of the Wisdom Tree: is that it?" Paul was beginning to get annoyed with Albert's longwinded story.

"A long time ago, many magical beacons like the Crimson Eye existed. Holding the staff is not enough to amplify one's own power: to channel power through the staff you first need a magical beacon like the one I have here," Albert held the Crimson Eye in front of him. "A few centuries ago, the Sorcery War gave rise to the Wizard Hunters: a sect of swordsmen who specifically targeted magic users. Many powerful spells were lost as a result of those Wizard Hunters, and many beacons were destroyed, making this gem rare indeed." Albert returned the stone to his pocket. "The beacon needs to sit atop the staff in order to use its power: one is useless without the other."

"Let me ask you this..." Paul leaned toward Albert. "What do you plan on doing with the staff once we bring it back?"

"That, my friend, is none of your business," Albert spat through his crooked smile.

"I don't know about this... who in their right mind would even *set foot* in the lair of a dragon?" Devon remarked.

"*That* is the exact reason I duped you two in the first place. No sane treasure hunter would set foot in there, and any skilled adventurer knows enough not to meddle with dragons." Albert rubbed his eyes with exhaustion. "I can obliterate the two of you: I've already made that clear. If you refuse to go: you die. If you go... well... you *might* die, but you might also emerge victorious. The choice is yours: I can, at the very least, give you that much."

The crooked man turned to leave: regardless of his anger, Paul did not stop him. He and Devon discussed at length what their options were and what the plan of action entailed. Paul came up with a plan to retrieve the staff. Even though he knew next to nothing about Red Dragons, Devon knew even less.

Retreat was not an option: if they were killed by the dragon, at least their deaths would be relatively quick. Something told them that Albert would be sure to make them suffer immensely, prolonging the process and taking some kind of twisted pleasure in their agony.

Sometime later, the two sat at a table discussing their plan of attack.

"All things considered, we really have no choice in the matter: we either do as he demands and *maybe* live to fight another day, or we can refuse, resulting in a most assured, and probably *very painful*, death." Paul observed.

Devon lowered his mug. "Well, the way I figure it, this is all just a game, so, why not play it?"

Paul stared back across the table. "Devon... are you stupid? The ale must have gone to your head already."

Devon once again broke away from his mug. "No: think about it. If resisting isn't in the cards, then why not stack the deck in our favor?"

Paul met Devon's suggestion with a blank stare.

"I'm talking about a map. Look, there's a master cartographer right in town: we might be able to ask him what he knows. With any luck, he'll have actually mapped the place out." Devon promptly drained his mug.

"Every time I think you're about to open your mouth and utter the stupidest thing I've ever heard, you prove me wrong. " Paul paused for a moment, then reached into his vest. "We should pool our remaining resources and stock up on supplies after we *hopefully* buy a map."

"Very well: but only after another round." Devon said, raising his arm to motion to the barkeep.

Paul rose from his seat. "No: let's keep our wits about us. We should go now, while it's fresh in our minds." he demanded, yanking Devon up by the arm.

"Alright, alright: you don't have to get so rough." Devon retorted.

"Yes, I do: the last time you said "just one more round", I ended up carrying you out of the tavern the next morning." Paul said flatly. "Now: where can we find this *'cartographer'*?"

"Why do you say it like that?" asked Devon.

"Because *'cartographer'* is usually a term used by con men to make themselves sound important: but a map maker is a map maker. Let's go: we're wasting time." explained Paul.

After paying off the hefty tab that the two of them racked up, Devon and Paul left in search of the cartographer. Unlike other well established professionals, and to their great suspicion, the "cartographer" had no shop to speak of: the map maker simply carted around his goods and could be found at various locations throughout town. He was, however, usually never in the same place twice in a row.

After searching the business district, the two found that the cartographer had been there two nights prior: eyewitnesses happened to see him carting his shop to the east, toward the theatre district. After a good deal of travelling and searching, the two found that they were, once again, too late in their quest. This time they were directed toward he town outskirts: apparently, the peddler frequented that area.

It was already late into the night when Paul and Devon made it to the outskirts of town. The two continued walking down a deserted alley when a cloaked man emerged from the shadows. Paul's hand instinctually moved to the hilt of his dagger.

"You boys picked a bad part of town to get lost in. You looking for something?" The cloaked man was surprisingly well spoken.

"You could say that..." Paul muttered as he eased his dagger out of the sheath, concealing it behind his arm.

"Lost at this time of night, and in a shady area on top of that. You're lucky you ran into me..." The stranger moved his hand to unclasp his cloak.

In the blink of an eye Devon had his sword out of the sheath.

"You boys need a map?" the stranger grinned.

"Do you have *any idea* how close Devon came to cutting you down?" shouted Paul.

"Happens more often than you'd think, kid." sighed the stranger. He was obviously the "cartographer" they were looking for.

"Let's get to the point... we need a map of the Red Dragon's lair in the Clarian Volcano. Do you have one?" Paul asked.

"Well, the thing about maps is that they're all about quality. To put it shortly: you get what you pay for." The Cartographer grinned.

"And here we go..." Paul whispered to Devon. "Ok, what's it going to cost?"

"These are hard to come by: I risked my neck to map that place out. It's a good map, so it won't come cheap. Let's say, 10, 000 Gold?" the map maker offered.

"10,000 is too high: that's more than we have between us. Lower your price." Paul negotiated.

"Alright, you two seem like nice boys: how about 9,000?" the strange man grinned.

"Still too high. Come on Devon: this fellow is obviously a fake." Paul turned to leave.

The stranger grabbed Paul by the wrist. "I can see that you two *really* want one of my maps. I'll tell you what: I usually don't do this, but you two seem like nice kids. I'll let you two have the map for whatever gold you have on you."

"But Paul, 8,000 gold pieces is all we have to our name." Devon blurted.

"8,000 eh? I'll take it." the map maker said excitedly.

The cloaked man produced a scroll that looked to be rather high quality from his pocket.

"I hope you're happy, Devon. Because you don't know when to keep your mouth shut, we won't have anything left for supplies." Paul took the map and shoved a pouch of gold towards the man's chest.

Paul anxiously unrolled the scroll to inspect what they had just paid for: it was indeed a map, but whether it was actually of the Clarian Volcano remained to be seen. "One more question..." Paul looked up.

The man who had sold them the map had vanished just as mysteriously as he had appeared.

"One way to find out about the map, eh?" Devon offered.

Paul looked down at the map. "Why do I have such a horrible sinking feeling?"

Chapter 13

Dead Heat

Though it was originally thought to be a mountain, the Clarian Volcano was renamed after it erupted and leveled the city that was built at its foundation. Parts of the charred stone wall that once surrounded the city could be seen peering out of the ground in certain areas: a constant reminder of the fiery doom that the volcano represented. Of course, it meant far more than that to Paul and Devon.

The two nervous adventurers stood at the base of the Clarian Volcano: the towering pile of magma and rock completely blocked out the sun. Though it was daylight outside by the time they arrived, the two stood in the shadows of twilight.

Paul unraveled the map of questionable origin and began looking for the best point of entry. Surviving this mad quest required two things: first, they would have to get in and out of the volcano with the staff. Second, their survival hinged on their avoiding the main nest where the Red Dragon had made itself at home.

After muttering something to himself and jabbing his finger at the map several times, he rolled it up and held the scroll out to Devon.

"Though I doubt the reliability of the map, the scroll indicates that the volcano is simply a series of caves. All we have to do is avoid the large chamber where the dragon has made its nest." Paul stretched and held the map back out to Devon. "Since this excursion will require more stealth and cunning than brute strength, I figured you are best suited to navigate the twisting caverns."

"Paul: I have a question..." Devon was cut off.

"It's very straight forward Devon: just keep your eyes on the map and we'll be fine." Paul chided.

"I see you're obviously not in a good mood, having to have to do this and all." Devon took the map from Paul's outstretched hand. "If it's as straight forward as you say, then let's get in and out of here as fast as possible."

Paul gestured to a rocky outcrop near a piece of charred wall. "According to the map, the entrance we want should be in-between those rocks over there."

Though Paul had doubted the map earlier, the entrance to the volcano was *exactly* where the scroll said it would be. Hot air and the fetid smell of rotting meat came out of the cave entrance in a wave. After a few moments, neither was sure if the smell had stopped, or if they simply became used to the stench.

After travelling down the first passage, Paul and Devon came to a fork that split into three paths.

"Alright Devon: which way is it going to be?" Paul asked.

Devon fiddled with the map for a moment, looking at it from different angles. "The path on the left..." he sounded more like he was asking a question.

"Are you certain? Because you don't sound confident." Paul sounded annoyed.

Devon inspected the map once again, this time, he held the map out in front of him as if to try to line the cave up with the map. "Left. Definitely left."

As per Devon's instruction, Paul led them down the left most path until they came to another fork in the cavern: one path heading left, and one path heading right. This time, after a quick inspection of the map, Devon pointed to the path on the right. A short trip down the corridor led them in a loop and spat them back out into the very same hallway with the fork.

"I thought you said right?" Paul asked.

"I did..." Devon said as he returned to checking the map. After a few moments of carefully scrutinizing the map, Devon came to the conclusion that he must have been looking at the wrong passageway. "I misread our location: I've got it now. If we head left, we ought to get where we want to be."

"You're sure this time?" Paul asked impatiently.

"Well, we can't go anyplace else, right?" Devon replied.

"Touché..." Paul trailed off.

Through Devon's lackluster navigational skills, and thanks to the process of elimination, the two were once again on the road to the staff within the volcano. A tremor followed by loosely packed dirt and small rocks falling from the ceiling stopped them in their tracks. The path that Paul marked on their map took them very far from the chamber of the Red Dragon, and though the Volcano hadn't erupted for a few decades, it was the only explanation that Paul could think of.

"Listen Devon: in a few minutes these halls might fill with molten rock, which would really hinder us considering we'd be dead. We really should move faster." Paul whispered.

Devon nodded and continued navigating the caverns using the map.

A few more turns took Paul and Devon to a dead end.

"How is this even possible?" Paul asked in disbelief.

"Don't look at me: I followed the map exactly like you told me to. I even followed the path that you marked off: see?" Devon extended the map to Paul.

"Devon... let me ask you something." Paul said calmly. "When you said 'I followed the map exactly': did you ever stop to think that *maybe* you were holding the map the wrong way?"

"I don't think so: no..." Devon replied.

"Devon... YOU WERE HOLDING THE MAP UPSIDE-DOWN, YOU IDIOT!" Pau's voice echoed through the caves.

"I had no way of knowing: there was no compass on the map, so I didn't know which way was up. I tried to tell you, but you kept cutting me off back before we entered the volcano. When you said it was straight forward, I just assumed you handed me the map right side up." Devon started to flinch away from Paul even though he was much larger.

Paul let out a large sigh. "So, the map probably was right the entire time."

His face went pale.

"What?" Devon demanded.

"If I marked the farthest path from the dragon on the map, and you were holding it upside down, that tremor we felt earlier..." Paul paused. "Change of plans: let's just get out of here. Facing an angry wizard is probably less frightening than facing an angry Red Dragon."

"But we don't know where we are. Remember, the map was upside down." Devon said hurriedly.

"It doesn't matter where we are: just backtrack!" Paul shouted.

Paul's shouting gave rise to another tremor: this time, a loud rumbling could be heard from deep within the cave. The two immediately began their hasty retreat from the volcano when they came upon the path that they had taken to get to that point. The tremor had caused a cave in, collapsing the path they had followed, but exposing two other pathways.

With little time to think, Paul led Devon down the path heading South: that cavern split into two more paths. Light could be seen coming from the path leading right, so Paul ran that way, hoping they had found the entrance: Devon ended up tripping over something even better.

Devon rose to brush the dust off of himself and see what he had tripped over. A wooden staff lay on the ground, almost completely obscured by dust and dirt. Devon slowly leaned over and picked the staff up.

"Is that what I think it is? If it is, then this entirely makes up for your mix up earlier." Paul marveled.

"It might be: Albert never actually told us *what* the staff looked like. But this *is* a staff guarded by a dragon: I somehow doubt it's a run of the mill staff." Devon observed with some sarcasm.

The cave began to shake fiercely: many of the large stones that lined the ceiling of the cave came crashing down around them. Behind them, the passage disappeared underneath a pile of debris just as quickly as it had appeared.

"Well: they say that 'burning bridges prevents retreat', or some rubbish like that. I guess the only way to go is forward. Besides, I can see light down this passageway." Devon said as he began to push forward.

Paul and Devon followed the straight path until it let out into a large chamber filled with the light of day.

"This doesn't seem right: are we on the other side of the volcano?" Paul mused.

Bones and other various animal carcasses littered the area. Silence filled the air as Paul and Devon scanned their barren surroundings for any immediate threats: the silence was broken by a deafening roar. The outline of a huge red creature stretched out behind a nearby hill: the two adventurers accidentally made their way into the Red Dragon's nest.

Chapter 14

Don't Play with Fire

"I think we've worn out our welcome..." Devon whispered: a pointless gesture since the beast was already well aware of their presence.

"We have an advantage in numbers: it'll have to choose which one of us to pursue." Paul answered, trying not to move.

"In other words, it has a choice of the order it devours us in..." Devon said with a face as stiff as a board.

As the two discussed among themselves the options that lay before them, the mighty Red Dragon approached them slowly, and rather clumsily. It was as if they had awakened the beast from a long slumber.

"Wait... do you see that?" Paul pointed at the dragon. "It's obviously still groggy, and it's far too large to give chase through the caverns."

"So what do you propose? If you have any ideas, you should share them now before that beast gets any closer." Devon shouted.

The lumbering beast was now within twenty feet of them.

"I *do* have one. RUN!" Paul broke into a sprint hugging the wall on the left of the dragon.

Devon took a moment to process the gravity of the situation and Paul's extraordinary feat of flight, but Devon, too, broke into a full run. To further throw the dragon off, Devon hugged the wall on the right.

The dragon, being much larger than either of the adventurers had imagined, stretched its tail out towards Devon and stretched it's neck out towards Paul. The creature easily struck the rock wall above both adventurers and sent down a rain of large, jagged stones to slow the egress of its prey.

Paul, being much more lithe than Devon, dodged around the falling rocks as he continued to run. Devon, on the other hand, was not quite as fortunate: his large frame, armor and the staff were a bit of an encumbrance when it came to mobility. As a result he was struck by several large rocks and his progress out of the nest was halted. Devon stood stuck between two boulders, with only a few feet on each side to move around. The rocks, unfortunately, were far too large to vault.

The dragon turned its body toward Devon and let out a deafening roar at its prey. The great beast lurched back and prepared to devour its target. As it reared back on its hind legs, the dragon bellowed once again: this time it was not a roar of anger, but a cry of pain.

Paul had driven his dagger into the soft underside of the dragon's tail. He withdrew his dagger and repeatedly plunged the blade into the soft flesh under the beast's tail: a vain gesture, considering the sheer size of the creature. He did, however, succeeded in drawing attention away from Devon.

Devon drew his sword and wedged the end of the blade beneath one of the rocks that blocked his escape: with a few pushes of his full weight, the boulder slid to the side just enough for Devon to squeeze by. As he ran across the giant, cavernous nest, he was struck in the back very forcefully. The blow sent him sprawling, knocking the wind out of his lungs in the process. Devon slowly regained his breath and pulled himself to his feet in order to continue his escape: he cast his gaze upward and saw that he was standing in the enormous shadow of the beast's muscular tail. The tail began it's very rapid descent.

The beast continually struck at Paul with its enormous jaws: the attacks repeatedly fell short of hitting their mark due to Paul's above average speed. Because he continually changed direction after each attack, Paul was now further from his target than he was when he made his desperate attack. Out of the corner of his eye, Paul saw something glistening in the light shining down from above the volcano. The glint was unmistakable: that was the shimmer that gold made when the sun hit it at the right angle. Seeing the hoard gave him and idea.

Devon raised his arms in an attempt to soften the blow from the dragon's tail, but was easily overpowered and was sent to his knees. The creature hammered Devon two more times: Devon was now prostrate and completely defenseless. The beast struck Devon once again before sweeping him to the side with a flick of its tail: the dragon turned to deliver the final blow and finish the first course of its meal, when a chalice struck the beast on the side of the head.

Paul stood on a pile of gold, throwing valuables and various trinkets around the cave. The dragon reacted as Paul had hoped, it ceased attacking the intruders and proceeded to collect and protect its hoard. The dragon turned to where Paul had thrown a large majority of the trinkets and scooped them up into its mouth: Paul took the momentary opportunity to run to Devon's aid.

"We have to be quick: that beast isn't going to be over there forever. Something tells me that it'll be hopping mad when it returns." Paul grunted as he hoisted Devon off of the ground.

"I really thought you were going to leave me behind while you escaped." Devon gasped.

"Truth be told: I thought about it for a moment. We're in this mess together to the end though. And between you and me, there were three things that really changed my mind." Paul began dragging Devon with one arm over his shoulder.

"And those things were?" Devon asked.

Paul was fast approaching he exit. "Well, number one: you were still holding the staff. Number two: if you managed to make it out of this volcano and you tracked me down, I was a good as dead anyway." Paul began to laugh.

"That's two..." Devon began to walk on his own as they passed into the safety of one of the caverns.

"Number three: I couldn't live with myself if I left you behind... probably. You have saved my skin quite a few times, after all. Now, as the saying goes, 'let's make tracks'." Paul laughed nervously.

Paul took the map out once again to try to deduce their location. He began talking to himself under his breath and pointing to various locations on the scroll.

"If the main nest is here, and we just came from there, then that must mean we're somewhere in this area..." Paul began running his finger around the map as he explained it to Devon. "That means: if we head in this general direction, we'll eventually end up outside. Hold onto this, and don't lose it." Paul handed the map to Devon.

The two adventurers walked in silence for some time.

"It's awfully dark in here: wouldn't you say?" Devon said, in an attempt to break the silence.

"We're in a cave inside a volcano: what did you expect? We've been in caves above and underground countless times: it shouldn't surprise you." Paul said grumpily.

"It doesn't: I was just trying to get you to cheer up." Devon replied.

Paul let out a small snicker: over time that snicker escalated into a full laugh. Devon's observation was so mundane and nonsensically stupid that Paul, despite his excellent poker face, could not help but laugh.

Twilight shone in from the entrance of the volcano, but neither one could tell if that was the actual time of day, or if that was the shadow cast by the volcano. As they walked out of the nightmarish cavern they saw that it was indeed dark out.

"We're out, and I don't know what I want to do more: eat, sleep, or get this staff to that crazy wizard so we can get out of this mess." Devon shouted.

"Isn't it obvious that we can do all three? We'll just hit the tavern." Paul answered: he was eager to end the contract with Albert.

"With what money? We spent everything we had on that map: remember?" Devon smiled and rolled his eyes at his own stupidity.

"Come on: who do you think you're talking to? Do you really think I'd stand on top of a pile of treasure without helping myself first?" Paul laughed as he withdrew a handful of gold from his pocket.

"Great! Now we have enough to... wait... You mean to tell me that you let me get pummeled while you were busy loading your pockets?" Devon yelled.

"But you're not dead..." Paul trailed off.

Devon shook his head and broke into a sprint: he chased Paul through the night and all the way back to the settlement where the mad wizard Albert waited for them.

Chapter 15

Heading Out on a Journey

"I said I was sorry." Paul insisted: he was once again in Devon's good graces. "We'll go to the tavern and you can eat and drink your fill: then we'll call it even."

"Maybe not *even*, but it'll do," laughed Devon: it seemed he was enjoying being the one in charge for a change.

It was late at night when the two arrived outside of the tavern: no doubt they'd find Albert waiting for them. Maybe it was timing, or maybe it was through some sort of magic, but that crooked wizard always seemed to know where Paul and Devon would be.

"So, what do you want to do after this job's over?" Devon asked, trying to make small talk.

"Well, I have no doubt that we'll run into that psycho tonight: once he frees us I'd say we take a small break from adventuring, maybe a week or so, and when we *do* look for new employment, no more wizards," Paul said, shaking his head.

"'Psycho'? Is that how you speak about your employer behind his back?" a voice rang out behind them, but by now, they knew who it would be.

Paul shut his eyes and sighed. "An employer *pays* you for your troubles." Paul said with his back still turned. "I think the term 'slave driver' is more appropriate for you." Paul turned towards the voice behind them: it was, to no surprise of his, Albert. "You know: it was eerie the first few times you tracked us down, but now I kind of expect it. You really should learn more tricks."

"I expect everything went swimmingly?" Albert said sarcastically.

"Well, we made it back alive with the staff: I wouldn't go as far as to say swimmingly, but we're alive," Devon said. Though he did not put his hand on the hilt of his sword, his muscles tensed, and he prepared for a potential conflict.

"The staff: give it to me," Albert said eagerly as he reached out to Devon.

"The contract first," Devon demanded.

"Give me the staff, then I'll give you the contract," Albert retorted.

"Show us the contract: we'll give you the staff, then you hand us the scroll," Paul insisted.

"Very well," Albert withdrew a scroll from his satchel. "Here it is, now: *hand it over*."

Devon started to hold the staff out to Albert.

"What are you, stupid?" shouted Paul. He reached up and took the staff from Devon. "Devon: I thought I taught you better than that. As far as *you* go: open that scroll up. I don't trust you."

Albert reluctantly opened the scroll. "You got me: that was a blank scroll. Here: this is the right one." The wizard withdrew yet another scroll and opened it up.: it was indeed the correct one.

Paul inspected the document to verify its authenticity. "Very well then: you hold out the contract, and when I give you the staff, you give me the scroll at the same time."

Albert and Paul then simultaneously exchanged articles: Paul promptly tore the contract to shreds. Albert then turned to leave.

"Not even going to tip us for our troubles, eh?" Devon joked.

"You're right... you went through all this trouble, after all. Here's your tip: never mess with a wizard!" Albert let loose a beam that struck Devon, enveloping him in light. "Take my advice: learn to use that sword of yours, because from now on, whenever you encounter any beast, you won't have a choice but to do battle."

Paul immediately ran to Devon's aid, although the warrior stood there seemingly unharmed. In fact, he felt better than he did a few moments ago. After seeing how Albert attacked Devon unprovoked, he allowed the wizard to leave without challenging him.

"Wizards..." Paul muttered as Albert walked off into the distance.

Devon shook off the shock of being hit by a strange beam, and the very first thing that came out of his mouth was "Well, I'm hungry. Let's go grab a bite to eat."

"Hm... You never cease to amaze me," Paul chuckled. "But you need to stop mentioning tips: it only seems to get us into trouble." Paul put his hand on Devon's shoulder and the two began their trip inside.

That night the tavern was livelier than usual: all manner of out of towners and adventurers seeking to make a quick profit were sharing drinks. Needless to say, Paul and Devon joined in the festivities: drinks flowed freely and stories were shared. Paul knew better than to believe some of the rants he heard though.

Midway through the night a competition started: one bar patron would make a bet with someone else, trying to best them and empty their gold pouch in the process. Like many bar bets, a majority of them required brute strength rather than brains: of course, Devon joined in. He participated in tests of fortitude, strength and dexterity: every victory filled his pouch with gold.

There was one fellow in particular that had bet himself destitute: he was the kind of man who seemed like he had absolutely no business competing with men like that. Luck struck again as the strange man had challenged Devon to a competition. As the rules dictated, since the other man issued the challenge, it was Devon's right to choose the terms of victory. Stranger still was what the man chose to bet: he put forward an old looking rope that he insisted had some magical property to it. Devon played along and wagered his entire gold pouch, and then issued a challenge he was certain he could win.

An arm wrestling competition.

The stranger, who was much smaller than Devon, foolishly accepted the challenge. Needless to say, Devon almost sent the small man crashing through the table when they squared off. Devon claimed his rather odd prize: on his way back to Paul's table, the strange man stopped him.

Meanwhile, Paul was invested in a lucrative sounding story: that is to say that he was eavesdropping yet again.

"Are you sure it was him?" a voice rang out at a nearby table.

"Sure I'm sure: only one wizard on Ringworld is that well known and powerful," said another voice.

"So you're sure. What'd he want anyway?" asked a third voice.

"Something about a Ruby Scepter. I didn't get to hear the whole offer," said the second voice again.

"I dunno about doing business with this guy. Didn't another wizard in town go mad with power and light himself on fire not even an hour ago. They say all that was left of him was this weird red orb-looking thing," said the first voice.

"Yeah: count me out. Living is more valuable to me than a whole mess of gold and magical items any day," the third voice said.

Paul's eyes lit up: a new job and with an employer who was likely to pay very well. It didn't matter to Paul that this chap hadn't asked him directly: if Paul showed up with the scepter, that was likely to be enough.

"Excuse me for prying, but this man who passed through here before: what was his name?" Paul posed the question to the entire table as he leaned over.

"I think his name was Duke, or something like that. He's apparently some kind of Master Wizard: or maybe some kind of sage. I forget which," one of the men said absentmindedly.

"Sorry to bother you: good day," Paul said, but what he really meant to say "thank you for letting me pull this job out from underneath you".

Devon approached the table with the old rope in hand. "Paul! You'll never guess what I just..." Paul promptly cut him off.

"Gear up Devon: we've got a new lead, and this time the reward is huge. The person we're retrieving something for is apparently of a very high status, which means we'll be set for a very, very long time," Paul said hurriedly.

"What are we retrieving?" Devon asked, refastening his armor.

"Something called 'the Ruby Scepter', Paul replied.

"Sounds like this will be a quick and easy job: let's go".

The End

www.ingramcontent.com/pod-product-compliance
Lightning Source LLC
LaVergne TN
LVHW050600160826
845677LV00011B/2393

* 9 7 9 8 8 4 3 7 4 4 8 8 5 *